A Storybook by Nancy E. Krulik
Based on the screenplay written by
Leo Benvenuti & Steve Rudnick and Timothy Harris & Herschel Weingrod

SCHOLASTIC INC.
New York   Toronto   London   Auckland   Sydney

12 11 10 9 8 7 6 5 4 3 2 1   6 7 8 9/9 0 1/0

Designed by Joan Ferrigno

Printed in the U.S.A.   09

First Scholastic printing, November 1996

Change was definitely in the air!

High-flying Michael Jordan, the world's greatest basketball player, had just announced he was leaving basketball . . . to become a baseball player!

And Michael wasn't the only one looking
for a change. Far off in the cosmos, a vicious
alien named Swackhammer was looking for ways
to spruce up his intergalactic amusement park,
Moron Mountain.

Maybe Swackhammer should have taken a close
look at Michael Jordan's new career.

After all, Michael wasn't exactly a shining star on the baseball diamond. His batting average was low, and his fielding was, well . . .

But Swackhammer was determined to make changes at Moron Mountain. He ordered the Nerdlucks, his alien slaves, to go out in search of new entertainers. Funny entertainers. Wacky entertainers. *Looney* entertainers.

So, the Nerdlucks crashed their spaceship into (where else?) Looney Tune Land.

As the aliens climbed from the wreckage, they met a gray-and-white guy with big ears. "We seek the one they call Bugs Bunny," a Nerdluck named Pound explained.

"Hmmm . . . Bugs Bunny? Say, does he have great big long ears, like this?" the gray guy asked, running his hands up and down his ears.

"Yeah," Pound nodded.

"And does he hop around, like this? Does he say 'What's up, Doc?' like this: 'Eh, what's up, Doc?'"

Pound smiled. "Yeah," he said.

The furry gray fellow took a bite of his carrot. "Nope, never heard of him."

You know, maybe there *is* no intelligent life out there!

Pound was stupid. But he wasn't *that* stupid. He eventually figured out that the carrot-chomping stranger was actually Bugs Bunny.

"Okay, Bunny. Gather up your Tune pals. We're taking you for a ride," Pound said, pointing his laser gun at Bugs.

Bugs gulped. This was an emergency.

Bugs immediately put out the word. It was time for an emergency Looney Tunes meeting!

The Looney Tunes were in the middle of an exciting cartoon when they got the call. Still they had no choice. They stopped right in the middle of the show and raced over to Town Hall.

"So what's the big emergency?" Daffy asked once all the Looney Tunes had arrived.

"All of you are now our prisoners. We are taking you to our theme park in outer space!" Pound declared.

Yosemite Sam jumped up and pulled out his pistols. "We ain't a-goin' nowheres!"

Pound took out his laser gun. With a flick of the trigger, Yosemite's guns disintegrated into dust. With a second flick of the trigger, Pound zapped Yosemite down to the size of . . . Tweety!

"Let's get them aboard the ship," Pound ordered.

Bugs jumped up. "Eh, not so fast, Doc. You can't just turn us into slaves," he explained. "That would be *bad*. You have to give us a chance to defend ourselves."

"Oh yeah? Who says?" Pound snorted.

Bugs pulled out a thin book called *Rules for Drawing Cartoon Characters* and pointed to a page. "Read 'em and weep, boys," Bugs said with a sly grin.

The aliens had no choice but to let the Looney Tunes defend themselves. After all, it *was* in the rule book.

But how *were* the Looney Tunes going to defend themselves? Everyone had a different idea.

How about we challenge them to a de-b-de-b-de-debate!

Say, we could have a bowling tournament!

"Okay, let's analyze the competition," said Bugs. "We got a small race of aliens . . ."

"Tiny little guys . . ." added Sylvester.

"Small arms . . . short legs . . ." Daffy pointed out.

"Can't jump high . . ." noted Porky.

Bugs looked directly at Pound. "We challenge you to . . ."

". . . a basketball game!"

"All right," Pound agreed. "Basketball it is." (Even though he didn't really know what basketball was.)

When Pound and the other aliens learned how the game was played, they knew they would have to study the moves of the pros and work hard in order to win. But the aliens were a lazy bunch. They never studied or worked hard at anything. So they decided to *steal* the pros' moves instead!

The aliens came up with a really sneaky plan. They
went to basketball games dressed as humans. They watched
as the players raced across the court — shooting, scoring,
and blocking shots. When they spotted a player whose style
they liked, the aliens released a purple ooze. Then the ooze
became a mist and traveled through the air and onto the
court.

The purple mist went straight into the brain of the
chosen player. Then the ooze made its way back to the
aliens, carrying the player's talent with it.

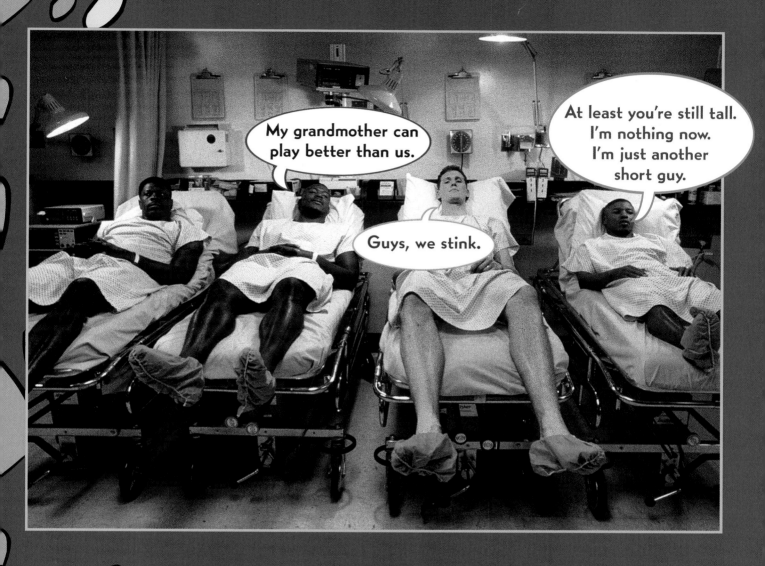

Before long, the Nerdlucks had captured the playing skills of Patrick Ewing, Charles Barkley, Larry Johnson, Shawn Bradley, and Muggsy Bogues.

Were the players sick? Nobody knew what was wrong. Even the doctors at the best hospital in the country couldn't figure it out.

There was only one great player left with his skills intact . . .

. . . Michael Jordan.
The aliens hadn't stolen Michael's basketball powers. Michael wasn't using his basketball powers. Michael was busy playing baseball . . . badly.

But no matter how badly he was doing, Michael was better off on the diamond than on the court. That's because there weren't going to be any professional basketball games for a while.

The basketball commissioner had just called a halt to the season until he could find out what was happening to his star players.

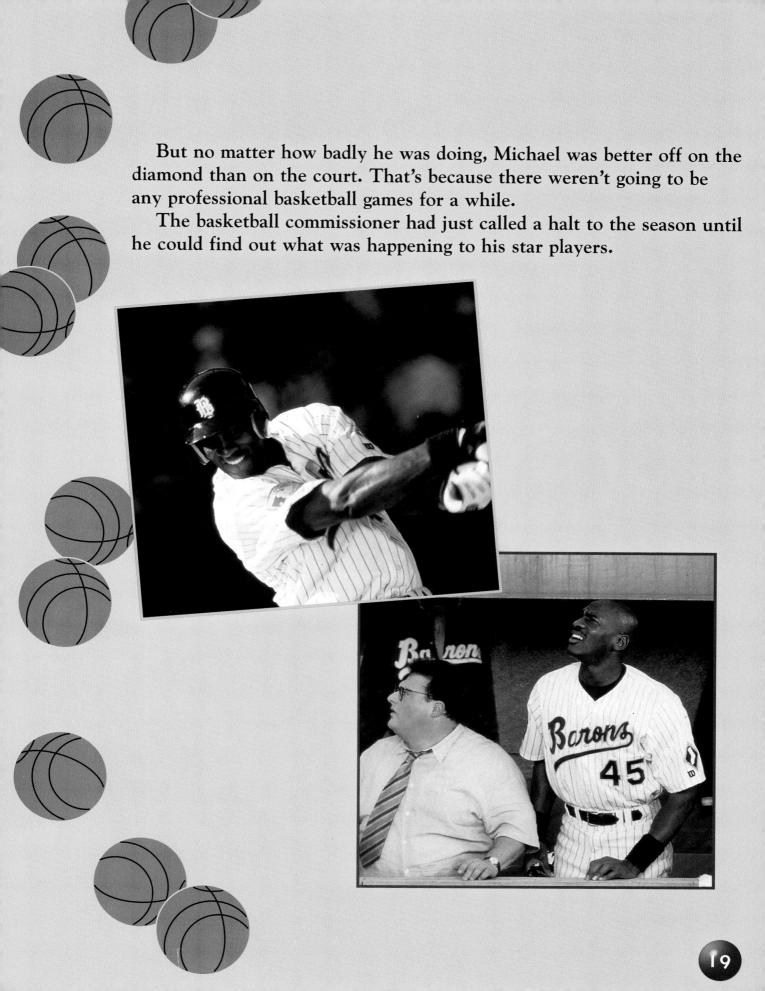

But the Looney Tunes weren't members of that league. *Their* big game was going to be played as scheduled.

"Coach, there's an important strategic question I need to ask you," Daffy said to Bugs during the team's afternoon practice.

Bugs looked up to discover Daffy modeling some wild team uniforms! "Whaddaya think?" Daffy asked. "I'm kind of partial to purple and gold myself. It goes better with my coloring."

Before Bugs could tell Daffy exactly what he thought, Porky came rushing onto the court. "The l-l-little aliens say it's their t-turn to use the court," the pig squealed.

The Nerdlucks raced onto the court. Daffy started to laugh. "Too bad you can't practice getting taller, boys," he said.

Daffy should have kept his mouth shut.

The aliens lined up in formation. Each little guy took out his own bottle of purple ooze. The Looney Tunes watched with disgust as the aliens raised the bottles to their lips and drank the sloppy, smelly goo.

I think we might need a little bit of help.

At first, there was a loud *BURP*. Then a purple gas surrounded the aliens. The aliens began to grow, and grow, and grow, until they towered threateningly above the Looney Tunes!

Those little pip-squeaks just turned into superstars . . .

Sufferin' succotash! They're *Monstars*!

While the Looney Tunes and Monstars were
busy practicing, Michael Jordan was enjoying
a relaxing game of golf with his pal Larry. Stan
Podolak had arranged the game. Stan worked with
Michael on the baseball team. Only Stan wasn't
a player — he was the guy who drove Michael to
and from the stadium. He also drove him nuts.

Michael watched as his pal Larry hit a beautiful drive onto the green. "You clowns can't beat that," Larry said assuredly.

That was all Michael needed to hear. He stepped up to the tee, swung, and unleashed a beautiful drive of his own.

The ball stopped about 40 feet from the hole. But just as the three men reached the ball, something incredible happened. The ball started rolling again — right in the direction of the hole. It was as though the ball had a mind of its own.

"That's impossible!" Larry said.

Impossible or not, the ball plopped right into the hole.

"All right!" Michael said, flashing his famous grin.

"Wait," Stan called over to Michael. "Let me get a picture of this. Reach in like you're going to get the ball. Now smile."

Michael reached in for the ball. He couldn't seem to grab it. He reached a little deeper. And a little deeper.

Suddenly, Michael was pulled all the way into the hole!

"Look out for that first step, Doc. It's a lulu!"

Michael Jordan rubbed his eyes in amazement. Was it possible, could this be . . . "Bugs Bunny?" Michael asked.

Bugs laughed. "You were expecting maybe the Easter Bunny?" he replied.

Michael gulped. "But . . . but . . . you're just a cartoon. You're not real."

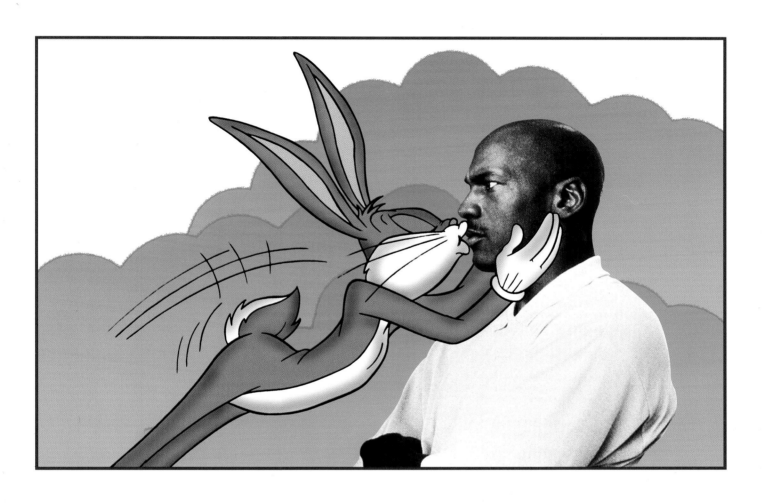

It was a challenge Bugs couldn't resist.
"Not real, eh? If I wasn't real, could I do this?"

Michael had to believe Bugs was real. It was too dangerous for him not to. "All right! All right! Enough already, you're real," Michael admitted. "But what . . . why . . . where?"

"You mean, What's up, Doc?" Bugs offered.

Bugs leaped onto Michael's lap. "Why Michael," he said, "I thought you'd never ask."

Bugs told Michael about the aliens who wanted to capture the Looney Tunes and take them to Moron Mountain. Then he explained about the upcoming basketball game. Michael's eyes grew wide as Bugs described the way the tiny aliens had morphed into giant Monstars.

"Am I getting through to you?" Bugs asked, finishing his speech. "They're going to make us do stand-up comedy — the same jokes every night — for all eternity. I'm talking about being trotted out to perform for a bunch of lowbrow, bug-eyed aliens. What I'm trying to say is . . . WE NEED YOUR HELP!"

"We got hoops!"
Daffy said.

Michael sighed. "But I'm a baseball player now," he explained to Bugs.

"Yeah. And I'm a Shakespearean actor," Bugs replied sarcastically. He led Michael into the Looney Tunes' gym.

"Look, I want to help," Michael told the Looney Tunes, "but I haven't played basketball in a long time. My timing's all off."

Bugs smiled. "We'll fix your timing," he said proudly. "Look at our facilities."

Michael glanced around. He was amazed by what he saw.

"We got basketballs!"
Sylvester shouted from
beneath the pile.

"We got weights!"
Taz added.

CRASH!

Before Michael could say anything, five huge, menacing Monstars came smashing through the stadium walls.

"Who are these guys?" Michael asked Bugs.

"Well, uh . . . remember the tiny aliens I told you about?" Bugs replied.

Pound wasn't waiting for Bugs to make any introductions. "We're the Mean Team," he sputtered at Michael. "We're the Monstars. Let's see what ya got, chump."

Pound fired a basketball right at Michael's head.

Michael grabbed the ball. "I don't play basketball anymore," he said, firing it back at Pound.

"Maybe you're chicken," Blanko said, challenging Michael.

I say! I resemble that remark!

35

Maybe Michael didn't play basketball anymore. But that didn't mean he couldn't *be* a basketball! Pound reached out and grabbed Michael. With one tight squeeze, Pound molded Michael into an NBA-size ball. Pound dribbled the Michael-ball a few times, then slam-dunked him into a basket!

"You're all washed up . . . baldy!" Bang bragged.

Michael Jordan could take having a ball fired at his head. He could take being slam-dunked through a hoop. In fact, Michael could take just about anything. . . . But when the big brutes knocked Tweety around, Michael had had enough.

A fierce look of determination came over Michael's face. "Let's play basketball," he announced to the Looney Tunes.

That night, Michael called his team together for an extra practice session. "Has anyone here ever played basketball before?" he asked.

Bugs blew a big, loud whistle. The whole team raced onto the court. Everybody tried to impress Michael.

Michael sighed. This team seemed hopeless. Then, a new player walked into the gym. "I'd like to try out for the team. My name is Lola Bunny," she said.

Bugs looked at Lola. His heart skipped — right out of his chest! "Hello. Eh . . . my name is Bugs," he introduced himself. "You want to play a little one-on-one, *DOLL*?"

Lola's eyes narrowed angrily. "On the court, Bugs," she ordered.

Bugs grabbed a ball, raced onto the court, and took a shot. Lola jumped up and blocked it. Bugs landed in a heap on the ground.

"Girl's got some skills!" Michael said.

Don't ever call me *"doll."*

Check!

Michael gave his first order. "Somebody is going to have to go to my house and pick up my basketball gear. And whatever you do, don't forget my North Carolina shorts!"

It was a tough job, but somebody had to do it.

So Bugs and Daffy raced over to Michael's house. They found his sneakers lying on the trophy room floor. Bugs grinned.

Maybe this job wasn't going to be so tough after all. The only thing left to do was find the shorts. Unfortunately, something was standing in their way . . . . Michael's bulldog, Charles.

Nice puppy. How about a bone!

Finally, Bugs and Daffy returned to the gym, sneakers and shorts in tow. They watched as Michael leaped high in the air and slam-dunked the ball in the basket. No doubt about it — Michael Jordan still had it.

Clap, clap, clap. Michael turned quickly to see who was applauding. It was Stan! "What are you doing here?" Michael asked him.

"I gotta take you back. You've got baseball practice."

Michael shook his head. "I can't right now. I'm helping my friends in their basketball game."

Unfortunately, so were the Monstars!
Everyone in the arena was tense — even the referee!
It was time for the tip-off.

Ready?

The referee tossed the ball in the air. Pound and Michael jumped. Michael tipped the ball to Bugs Bunny, who . . . just stood there!

"I got it. I got it. I got it!" Bugs cried as he held the ball tightly to his chest.

The Monstars charged right at Bugs! "Coming through, little boys," Nawt snarled. He grabbed the ball from Bugs. Then Blanko hammered Bugs into the court like a skinny, gray-and-white nail.

Almost the entire Tune Squad froze in fear. Only Lola and Michael seemed able to move. It was up to them to guard the whole Monstar team. It wasn't an easy task.

Nawt raced across the court. The mega Monstar leaped into the air and . . . *SWISH!*

The Monstars were really in a groove! They shot! They scored! They slammed Looney Tunes to the ground!

By the end of the first half the score was:

MONSTARS 64   LOONEY TUNES 18

The Tune Squad made their way back into the locker room. Their faces almost dragged across the floor.

Moron Mountain, here we come!

The Monstars, on the other hand, raced back into their locker room, cheering all the way! Swackhammer was there to meet them. "Not bad for the first half," he told the Monstars, "but we gotta keep this up."

"Hey, no problem," Pound said.

"We stole the talent from the best players in basketball," Nawt explained.

The Monstars were sure the game was in the bag. But the Monstars hadn't counted on the Tune Squad's secret weapon . . .

Stan Podolak!

Shut up! I smell something.

It smells like . . . a spy!

Uh . . . we have been playing really hard.

Stan had snuck into the Monstars' locker room, hoping to find the secret to their success! And after hearing Pound and Nawt, even a numskull like Stan could figure out what had happened. Stan Podolak was now the only person in the world who knew what had happened to the star players' talent! He rushed back to the Looney Tunes' locker room to reveal the Monstars' secret!

"The Monstars," Stan wheezed. "They stole the talent from the pros!"

Now Michael knew just what to do. He had to play as though he were up against other pros. And there wasn't a professional alive who could beat Michael Jordan!

Michael felt really pumped. He gave his team a little pep talk. "Listen up. I didn't get dragged down here to get whipped by a bunch of ugly Monstars! We've got to fight back. We've got to get right in their faces."

It was a very passionate speech. Too bad nobody heard it.

Bugs Bunny had one of his brilliant ideas. He grabbed a water bottle and filled it to the top. "Great speech and all, Doc," he complimented Michael, "but, eh, didn't you forget something? Your secret stuff?"

Michael had no idea what Bugs was talking about.

"*You* know, your secret stuff," Bugs said again. Bugs winked at Michael. Bugs took a big swig from the bottle. Almost instantly he turned into a muscle man.

"You wouldn't hold out on us, wouldya?" Sylvester asked Michael, his voice pleading. He grabbed the bottle and took a swig.

"I . . . no . . . I didn't think you guys really needed it," Michael said. "I mean, you're so tough . . . you're competitive."

"We're also chicken, son," Foghorn Leghorn admitted as he took a sip.

It was time for the second half of the game. The referee
blew his whistle and tossed the ball. The Monstars were
ready to sweep the floor with the Tune Squad. But Michael
Jordan and the Tune Squad were ready to stop them.

Suddenly, from the far corner of the gym came a loud,
bellowing, frightening howl.

"TIME OUT!!!!!!!!!"

The mighty Monstars quaked in their sneakers. The voice belonged to the person they feared most — their boss, the evil Swackhammer!

Swackhammer strutted onto the court and slammed Pound.

"Why didn't you get *this* guy?" Swackhammer asked, pointing to Michael.

"Because he's a baseball player," Nawt explained.

"He looks like a basketball player to me," Swackhammer said.

"He's the one I want for Moron Mountain."

Michael laughed. "Hey," he called over to Swackhammer. "You want a piece of me? Come and get it. How about we raise the stakes a little? If *we* win, you give the pros their talent back. If *you* win, you get me."

Swackhammer looked at his mean, lean Monstars. Then he looked at the wimpy Tune Squad. It was an offer he couldn't refuse! "Crush 'em!" he shrieked.

The game resumed. And this time the Monstars would stop at nothing to win.

One by one, the Monstars destroyed the Tune Squad.
They slammed Daffy . . .

. . . pounded Porky . . .

. . . and trampled Taz!

All the while, Michael was scoring. But he knew he needed help. The Tune Squad was down to four players on the court. They needed five to play. Unfortunately, all of their substitute players were injured.

If they didn't find a fifth player, the Tune Squad would have to forfeit the game. And Michael Jordan would become Moron Mountain's newest attraction!

Then, Michael spied his fifth player sitting alone on the bench. The Tune Squad's secret weapon — Stan Podolak! "Stan, you're in at center!" Michael told him. Now Michael had all the players he needed. They could start playing again.

But first, Daffy had a question. "You got any more of that secret stuff?" he asked. "I think it's starting to wear off."

Michael smiled. "It didn't wear off," he said. "It was just water. You guys had the special stuff inside of you all along."

The Tune Squad lined up on the court. Michael looked at his teammates. They were a mess. A sorry mess. (All except Stan, but he had his own problems.) Still, at least there were five of them.

"Just guard the big guy," Michael told Stan.

"Guard him? I'll smother him," bragged Stan.

Unfortunately, the only one who got smothered was Stan. Luckily, just before the Monstars flattened him into a pancake, Stan managed to shoot the ball at the hoop.

Michael watched as the ball soared through the air and went through the basket. *Amazing!* But not nearly as amazing as what happened next.

Foghorn raced onto the court with a spatula. Then he scraped up the Stan-cake and flopped him onto a stretcher.

Before long, Stan looked human again. (Well, as human as someone like Stan could look.)

"How'd he do that?" Michael asked.

Anybody could do that, Doc! Even *you*! This is Looney Tune Land!

Michael looked at the scoreboard. The Monstars were winning by one point. The Tune Squad had a chance — if they could find a player to replace the injured Stan.

"*Beep beep!*" Just then, Road Runner raced onto the court! All right!

"We've only got ten seconds," Michael told his teammates. "They have the ball. We go for the steal." Michael grabbed the ball and leaped into the air.

The Monstars weren't going to let His Royal Highness fly! They rose up high. A sea of Monstar arms and bodies blocked Michael's way.

Now if this had been a professional game, Michael would have been finished. But *this* was a Looney Tunes game. And when in Looney Tune Land, you do as the Looney Tunes do. Michael stretched his body like a giant cartoon rubber band. He wound himself right around the Monstars, and jammed the ball into the basket!

Buzzzz! The crowd cheered as the game ended. The Tune Squad had won! Michael and the Looney Tunes would not have to go to Moron Mountain after all.

But the Looney Tunes weren't the only ones who didn't want to go to Moron Mountain. The Monstars didn't want to go, either. They were sick of Swackhammer's bullying. The Monstars circled around Swackhammer. Together, they strapped him to an ACME rocket and launched it out of the stadium . . . out of Looney Tune Land . . . out of the galaxy!

Then the Monstars gave Michael back his friends' basketball powers.

Michael raced over to the local gym. He found his buddies long-faced on the court.

"So, I hear you guys want your games back . . . what little games you had to begin with," Michael teased. He held out a glowing, purple basketball.

"Come on. Touch it. Put your hands on it."

The guys were a little nervous, but they did as Michael said.

And suddenly all was right with the world. Swackhammer was floating through space. The Looney Tunes were back on TV. The star players were stars again. And Michael Jordan was back where he belonged — on the basketball court.